Flamingo Dream

BY **DONNA JO NAPOLI**

ILLUSTRATED BY
CATHIE FELSTEAD

GREENWILLOW BOOKS
An Imprint of HarperCollinsPublishers

Flamingo Dream
Text copyright © 2002 by Donna Jo Napoli
Illustrations copyright © 2002 by Cathie Felstead
All rights reserved. Printed in Singapore by Tien Wah Press.
www.harperchildrens.com

The full-color art was prepared as collages created from a variety of materials.
The text type is Leawood Medium BT.

Library of Congress Cataloging-in-Publication Data
Napoli, Donna Jo, (date)
Flamingo dream / by Donna Jo Napoli ; illustrated by Cathie Felstead.
    p.   cm.
"Greenwillow Books."
Summary: Grieving over her father's death from cancer, a young girl celebrates
their last year together by making a book that includes mementos and a story.
ISBN 0-688-16796-9 (trade). ISBN 0-688-17863-4 (lib. bdg.)
[1. Death—Fiction. 2. Fathers and daughters—Fiction.] I. Felstead, Cathie, ill.
II. Title.   PZ7.N15 Fl 2002   [E]—dc21   2001023072

1 2 3 4 5 6 7 8 9 10 First Edition

Last summer Daddy and I flew through clouds.
The pilot gave me a pin with little wings.
Daddy said, "They look like your wings."
I twisted hard and looked over my shoulder.
"I don't see wings."
"They're just buds now," said Daddy. "But
they are growing."

We went to visit the place in Florida where
Daddy grew up. We stayed with Aunt Catherine,
Daddy's sister. We picked hibiscus flowers from
her yard. Daddy taught me how to break off
the bottom and slowly pull out the little thread
and suck the sweet drop. He tucked flowers
all through my hair, everywhere everywhere.
Daddy said, "You're sprouting feathers."
Later I pressed the flowers in our big
old dictionary.

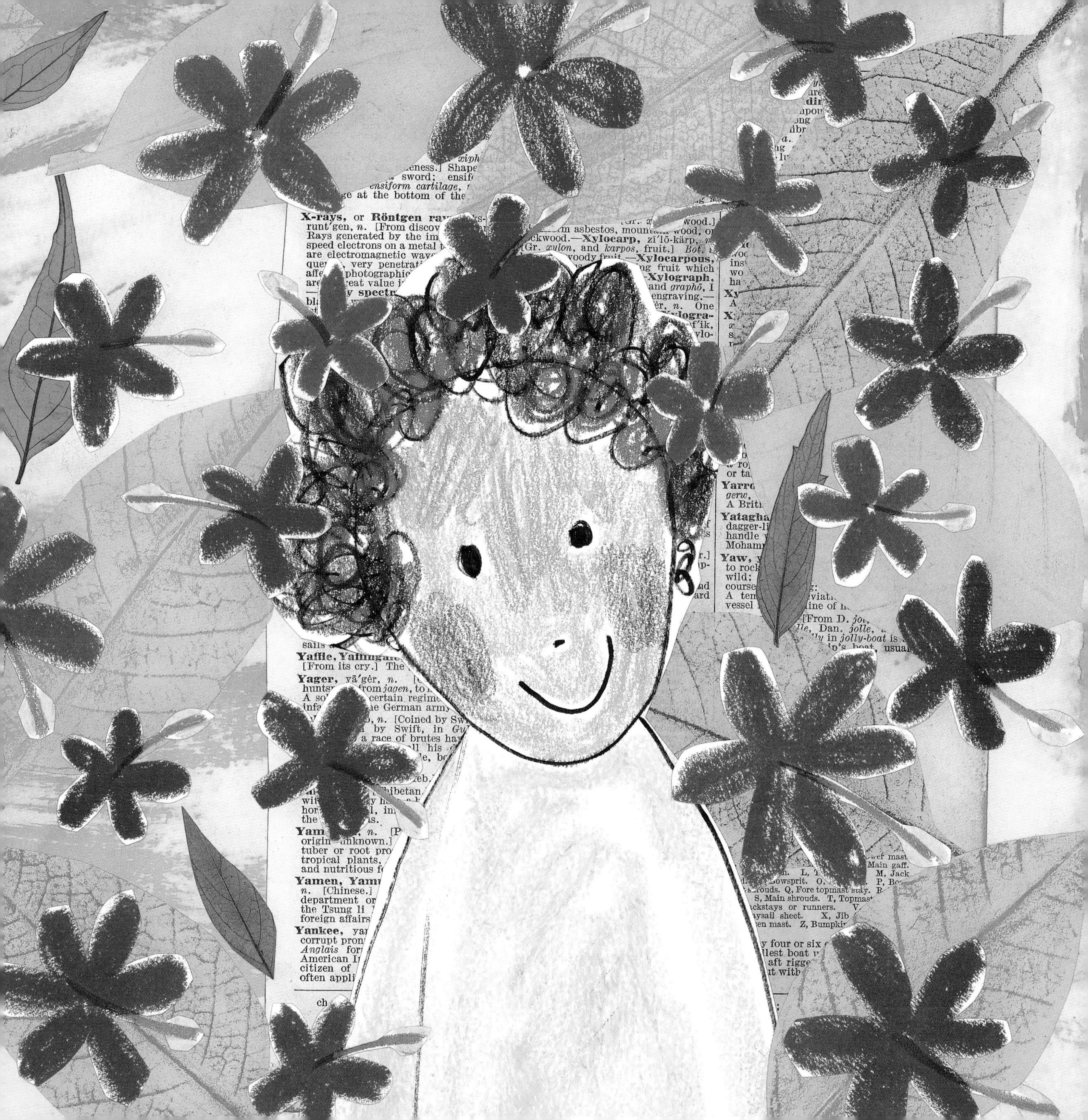

When Daddy was a kid, his father took him to the dog racetrack. They used to go early in the morning, just to walk and talk. On this trip Daddy took me to the racetrack. Daddy sat on the bleachers while I scouted around for betting stubs.

Daddy showed me the mechanical rabbit. It goes on an inner rail, and the dogs chase it around the track. Daddy told me that once he saw a dog jump onto the grass in the center and run across the green to the other side of the track. The dog caught the rabbit as it came around.

I could imagine that smart dog feeling so proud. I watched the flamingos walking through the pond on the green. "What did the flamingos do when the dog ran by?"

"They flapped like crazy and smashed into each
 other," Daddy said.
I ran in circles, flapping my arms.
"That's exactly how they ran," said Daddy. "Are
 you maybe a flamingo at heart?"
"Why didn't they fly away?" I asked.
 Daddy rubbed his upper arms and thought about
 that. "Some people say flamingos can't fly. But
 my money's on motivation."
"What do you mean?"
"Well, they wouldn't really want to fly away.
 Flamingos know that Florida is the best place
 to be in winter."
I stuffed pink-and-white feathers in my pockets.

We went to the beach.

And the parrot jungle.

And the monkey jungle.

We went to the movies on Miracle Mile.

Everywhere we went, Daddy said,

"I loved this place when I was a kid."

And everywhere we went, I answered,

"And I love it now."

Hello

Once Daddy had to go to the hospital for therapy.
I held a cold cloth on his forehead afterward
because he felt so bad. I did everything for him
that Mamma did when we were at home.
When we left Florida, Daddy and I both wore
shirts with pink flamingos all over, front and
back. I leaped up the steps into the airplane.
Daddy said, "Just a little higher and you'll fly."
Then he whispered, "Thank you, little bird.
Thank you for making this trip the best ever."
I saved our boarding passes.

The very next day school started. Mamma walked me there every morning. I made friends and played counting games and listened to stories.
I drew lots of letters
and learned how to play marbles
and made spitballs.

And every afternoon I came home to Daddy.
He sat on the couch and pointed out the
window and told me what he had seen happen
in our yard that day. Then I showed Daddy
what I had learned. He listened closely.
I had so much to say that sometimes
Daddy fell asleep listening.
Mamma and Daddy and I talked about
his cancer. Mamma said that Daddy was
changing inside, just as the leaves were
changing color. She said he would die,
just as the leaves would fall. Sometimes
we cried together, all three of us.

One day Mamma came early
to get me from school. She told
me Daddy was in the hospital.
I knew that would happen. Mamma
had told me that when Daddy got
too sick to stay home, he'd go to
the hospital.
I put on my flamingo shirt over my
sweater, and we went to see him.

Daddy's eyes were shut. Mamma told me he was in
a strange sleep, and maybe he could hear. She talked
to him just like normal.

Then she sang to him.

Then she hummed. Tears wet her cheeks. I sat on the
edge of his bed. I told Daddy I was wearing the flamingo
shirt he bought me. I told him I would always remember
our last trip together.

Then I ran my fingers across the back of his quiet hand.
I wanted him to wake up so much, it was hard not to
shake him. But I knew he needed to sleep. "Dream,"
I said into his ear. "Dream."

The next day Daddy died. Mamma gave me the plastic
identification bracelet they had put on his wrist in the
hospital.

Daddy's friends came to the service. They said he was sleeping peacefully. They talked about all the funny things he had done. They pulled on my curls. They brought boxes. In each box was a pink flamingo. Daddy had told them to bring me flamingos when he died. I put the flock of flamingos in the front yard so that I could see them when I sat in Daddy's spot.

I told Mamma, "Daddy's sleeping peacefully. When he wakes up, he won't even remember he died."

Mamma held me close. "Daddy will never wake up. That's what it means to be dead."

Mamma put the urn with Daddy's ashes on the mantel. I sat on the couch and tried not to look at it. I looked out the window instead.

The flamingos looked back at me. But I knew their eyes couldn't see. I ran outside and knocked them over. "You're dead," I shouted. "You'll never wake up. Don't pretend."

For a week the flamingos lay on their sides in the dry grass. They looked like junk.

Then one day I saw a big fat cat asleep, curled in the loop of a flamingo. I chased it away. I carefully stood up all the flamingos.

An idea came to me—and Mamma agreed. We scattered Daddy's ashes in the grass around the flamingos' legs.

"Take care of him," I whispered.

And I cried. I cried all day. I cried even when I was sleeping.

That was a month ago.

Yesterday it snowed hard. Mamma said my flamingos were lost in the snow. I looked out the window, and I couldn't see them. I was sad.

But last night I dreamed a flapping storm of pink. And when I woke, I was happy. My flamingos aren't lost. I know exactly where they went—back to Florida for the winter. And they took Daddy with them. I miss him. I think about him a lot.

Daddy loved his camera. He took so many pictures.

Every year on my birthday he spread out the pictures from that year. Then he chose a handful to put in a book, just for me. He called it my Year Book. And we wrote a story to go with the pictures.

I don't have a camera. But I collect things.
Today is my birthday. I've been working on
this book since dawn.
I show it to Mamma.
"See the wings and the hibiscus and
the betting stubs and the feathers
and the boarding passes and
the hospital bracelet?"

"You made your own Year Book." Mamma smiles.
"That's just what Daddy would have wanted. Are
you ready to write the words now?"
Yes. I know the story I want to tell.